Disconnect

D0710982

Disconnect

Lois Peterson

Orca currents

ORCA BOOK PUBLISHERS

Copyright © 2012 Lois Peterson

All rights reserved. No part of this publication may be reproduced
or transmitted in any form or by any means, electronic or mechanical, including
photocopying, recording or by any information storage and retrieval system now
known or to be invented, without permission in writing from the publisher.

Library and Archives Canada Cataloguing in Publication

Peterson, Lois J., 1952-
Disconnect / Lois Peterson.
(Orca currents)

Issued also in electronic formats.
ISBN 978-1-4598-0144-8 (BOUND).--ISBN 978-1-4598-0143-1 (PBK.)

I. Title. II. Series: Orca currents
PS8631.E832D58 2012   jC813'.6   C2012-902225-X

First published in the United States, 2012
Library of Congress Control Number: 2012938149

Summary: Fourteen-year-old Daria's addiction to technology
creates serious problems in her life.

*Orca Book Publishers is dedicated to preserving the environment and has
printed this book on paper certified by the Forest Stewardship Council®.*

Orca Book Publishers gratefully acknowledges the support for its
publishing programs provided by the following agencies: the Government
of Canada through the Canada Book Fund and the Canada Council for the Arts,
and the Province of British Columbia through the BC Arts Council
and the Book Publishing Tax Credit.

Cover photography by Getty Images

ORCA BOOK PUBLISHERS
PO Box 5626, Stn. B
Victoria, BC Canada
V8R 6S4

ORCA BOOK PUBLISHERS
PO Box 468
Custer, WA USA
98240-0468

www.orcabook.com
Printed and bound in Canada.

15 14 13 12 • 4 3 2 1

R0427324851

*For teachers and students at the
South Surrey/White Rock Learning Centre.*

Chapter One

"Are you listening?"

I typed, **In case I forget later, GL with the dance comp. Gotta go.**

"Daria!"

"Okay. Okay!" I said as I hit *Send* and pocketed my phone.

"I told her you would go by after school," my mother said. "To meet the kids."

"Told who?" I asked through a mouthful of cereal. "What kids?"

I looked up from the table when I noticed the silence filling the kitchen. My mother's hands gripped the chair in front of her. Her eyes were closed.

"What?" I asked. So now she expected me to read her mind?

Mom opened her eyes. Her hands were white on the top of the chair. "Why do I waste my breath?" she hissed.

"What?" I asked again. I scooped up a spoonful of cereal and munched.

Mom sighed. "Cynthia Clarkson. A colleague of mine? I have told you about her." My mother must be the only person who can spit through clenched teeth. "She has two children," she said. "They need a babysitter."

"Me?" Only twelve-year-olds babysat!

"This would be one way to earn the fare to see Selena and Josie at spring break," she said.

"I want to work at the mall," I told her. "In a clothes store, maybe. So I can get a discount."

"You're too young to work in retail."

My phone vibrated against my leg. I pulled it out of my pocket and checked the screen. Two messages.

"Leave that," said Mom. "Listen to me for one minute."

"I am listening." One was a text from Josie. **Call S to wish her luck. PLS. Shes driving me nuts.**

Mom's hand shot out and batted the phone from my hand. It skittered across the table.

I grabbed it and wiped it on my shirt. "You could have smashed that!"

Suddenly my mother's face was so close I could see the pores on her nose. "Give me your attention," she said. "For once."

"Chill out, would you?" I checked the screen to make sure everything still worked.

"That's it. Forget it." Mom shoved her chair hard against the table, causing my spoon to tip out of my bowl and clatter onto the floor. "I thought it would be a good idea," she said. "Just forget it."

"Mom!" Why did she have to over-react to everything?

"Never mind. I'll be late. Clean up that mess," she said as she charged out.

I watched the door, expecting her to come back. She sometimes does that. She gets a second wind and starts in again at full rant.

When I heard Mom's footsteps thud up the stairs, I settled back in my chair. I quickly texted Josie back. **Did already. U kno S. Tell her to imagine Im there watching. Take pics.**

I closed my phone and stuck it in my pocket.

Babysitting! What was Mom thinking? Snotty kids. Reading stories. Doing puzzles! There had to be better ways to make the fare back to Calgary.

Chapter Two

I sat next to the window in case things got boring, and in the middle row to avoid getting noticed. I unpacked my books and binders and stacked them on my desk with my phone on top.

"Okay if I sit here?" asked a girl I'd never seen before. She was wearing a knitted hat with pink strings that hung down to her shoulders.

I shrugged.

The girl unloaded her bulging green bag and unpacked a load of stuff onto the desk. "I love the first day at a new school." A silver ring in her bottom lip flickered. "I'm Cleo." She stuck her hand across the aisle.

"Pleased to meet you." I kept my own hands on my desk.

Cleo didn't seem to notice the snub. "And you are?"

"Daria. Rhymes with malaria." Josie had pointed that out the day we met in grade two.

Cleo pulled a pen out. "I just moved to Delta. What's it like, then?"

"Boring."

"I guess you'd feel that way if you always lived here," said Cleo.

"We got here last month."

"Maybe we should check out town together," she said.

"I don't think so." I picked up my phone and clicked through my messages.

"That's a cool phone," said Cleo.
Cool? It was at least a year old.

I was reading another panicked text from Selena when the classroom noise died down. Bags thudded to the floor, chairs scraped and the talking subsided.

Mr. Jenks swung around from scribbling on the board. "I have your attention. Good." He scanned the room. "Class. We have a new student joining us. This is Cleo Bennis."

"Hello, all." Cleo grinned and waved. You'd have thought she was the Queen.

Snickers came from behind her. A few kids muttered "Hi" as if they couldn't care less. But no one waved back.

Keep your head down and mind your own business, I thought. Works for me.

Cleo was right behind me as everyone swarmed out of the room after class. "So how about it?" she asked.

Going for gold!!! Wish u were here.

I looked up from Selena's message. "How about what?"

"Checking out the neighborhood?" Cleo's hat strings bobbed as she jostled her way through the door.

"I have to go straight home," I told her. I sounded like a kindergarten kid, so I added, "I'm babysitting tonight." As if.

Cleo's smile faded. "That's fine. Okay."

I almost felt bad.

"What class have you got next?" Cheerful again. "I've got honors math." She tapped her schedule against her cheek. "Where is room nineteen?"

"Second floor. Next to the girls' washroom. I'm headed the other way." I pushed through the crowd, head down, my eyes on my phone screen.

I could feel Cleo watching me. But I didn't turn back.

At the Kave, a guy with green hair sneered, "We don't hire babies." At Bookends, they asked for ID. I told the McDonald's manager, whose name tag said his name was Cliff, that I was fifteen. He gave me an application form and told me to return it with my birth certificate.

It was the same in every store. Even to stock shelves, you had to be fifteen. I had seven months to go. I shoved the McDonald's paperwork into the nearest garbage can.

Back home, Josie and Selena and I hung out at the Chinook Center after school most days. We would share an iced cappuccino while we scoured the sales racks at The Gap and checked out the movies and CDs at HMV. Sometimes we did our homework at the food fair. We weren't total slackers.

When we started high school together, we came up with a Cool Code of Conduct. One: Keep your head down.

If you're invisible, you can get away with almost anything. Two: Don't fail. It was like being a fish, Selena said. Slow down, and an eagle swoops down and grabs you. She's into nature big-time. Three: Stick together. High school—and life—are hard enough. The only way to survive is to stay connected.

Since my parents dragged me to Delta, the old rules worked. Especially number three. Even with a thousand kilometers between us, Selena, Josie and I were never out of touch.

When I checked my phone, I had three messages. One panicked one from Selena. Another from her. And one from Mom.

I checked that first. Selena's performance nerves were getting boring. It was always the same.

Home by 5. Pls.

Wots up? I texted Mom back. Then started one to Selena. **Good luck. #? do I have to say it? Break a leg etc.**

I didn't notice the old lady until she barged into me. I grabbed her shopping cart to regain my balance. "Sorry."

"It's my fault." Two harsh dark lines were drawn above the woman's eyes where her eyebrows should have been. "My daughter said I wasn't ready," she said. "But a short walk around the mall, I told her. How could that hurt?" One of her legs was encased in a blue Aircast.

"Are you okay?" I asked.

"No blood spilled." The woman smiled. "Not bad news, I hope."

"Pardon me?"

"You were so intent on your phone." The woman eased herself down onto the bench.

"I was checking on my friends."

"You're meeting up with them, I expect," she said. "You better get on."

"No. They're back in Calgary. One has a dance recital tonight. I was texting to wish her good luck."

The woman nodded. "My grandsons do a lot of that. I hardly get a word out of them when they visit."

Another text alert beeped. "I better get going," I said.

"You go ahead. Nice to meet you." The woman pulled her shopping cart close. "I'll just sit here for a bit."

I was heading out the door by Safeway when I saw Cleo coming my way, loaded down with grocery bags. Striped mittens swung from her sleeves. "I thought you were babysitting," she said.

I felt myself flush. "I'm headed there now."

"I could walk you."

"I'm in a bit of a rush."

As I stood on the sidewalk waiting for the light to change, I realized that it wasn't my sparkling personality that Cleo was interested in.

She was new too. She didn't have any friends here and thought I might do.

I already had all the friends I needed. Even if they were miles away. And one was having another meltdown.

Chapter Three

I finally gave in to Mom's nagging and decided I would babysit for her friend. My real motive was knowing it would take more than my stingy allowance to get back to Calgary.

On my first visit to meet the kids, they looked sweet, sitting at the table.

"This is Emmy," said Ms. Clarkson. The girl's hair was red and curly. "And this is Caden." His mom ruffled his straight hair. "Sit down, please. Can I get you a snack?"

"I'm fine, thanks, Ms. Clarkson."

"Call me Cynthia."

"Do you got LEGO?" Caden asked me.

"That's all he thinks about," Emmy said.

"I still have mine from when I was little," I told Caden.

He grinned at me. "Do you want to see my space station?" He slid down from his chair and darted from the room.

"He will make you look at it, even if you don't want to." Emmy rolled her eyes. "It is his pride and joy, that's what Mommy says. I don't have a pride and joy."

"Is Emmy short for Emily?" I asked.

"It's Emerson." The little girl got down from the table. "Not all Emmys are called Emily, you know." She stood with her hands on her hips. "We have a Ping-Pong table downstairs. Can you play?"

"Daria is going to visit with me for a while," said her mother.

"After, then?" asked Emerson.

"I don't expect she can stay long this time."

My hand itched to wrap itself around the phone. At least five calls had come in since I got to the house. Mostly from Selena, who had only placed bronze in jazz dance and was having a major pity party.

But I did want this job. "I can play for a little while," I told Emmy. "But I'm not very good."

"I am," said Emmy as she danced out of the room.

"So." Ms. Clarkson drank the dregs of Caden's milk. "I need you Tuesday, Thursday and Friday. From two forty-five until about six. Three hours a day, three days a week."

You didn't have to be in honors math to figure out that was more than three hours a day. "That's fine," I answered. I could bring it up later. "Do I have to pick them up at school?"

"There's a car pool," said Cynthia. "But you must be here when they get dropped off."

"Sure."

"I am looking for someone reliable," she continued. "Basically, you give them a snack, let them watch no more than an hour of TV. They play well on their own. And together."

"Sounds good."

"Emmy is pretty steady," Cynthia told me. "But keep an eye on Caden. He gets into mischief. But nothing too serious. So Tuesday, Thursday and Friday? How is eight dollars an hour?"

Twenty-four bucks a day. Seventy-two a week. How much would that be a month?

Not as much as retail, maybe, but enough to start saving for a trip home. "That's fine."

I was hardly out the door before I was on my phone to Selena. **There's always next time. Kno wot? I got a job!! Babysitting 2kids. WDYT?**

I had babysitting figured out by my third time. Paper and crayons and scissors kept Emerson happy for hours. Caden was more work. He was always bugging me to "Watch this," "See what I can do?" or "Come and play."

Today he kept leaning over to stick his head between mine and my phone while I tried to talk to Josie.

Cs cute. But his sister is way easier. Any tips? Josie has a rash of small cousins.

"Daria."

R all boyz a pain? I hit *Send* and watched the screen for Josie's reply.

"Daria!"

"What?" I nearly caught Caden with my elbow as I turned toward him.

He shoved his juice box at me. "I hate apple juice. It smells like sick. Doesn't it smell like sick, Emmy?"

"It's called vomit, if you must know," she told him. "I like apple better than orange." She dropped her empty juice box into the recycling bin.

"Vomit. Vomit. Vomit," crowed Caden. He crammed the last cracker in his mouth. "Vomitvomitvomitvomit," he chanted as he dashed out of the room and up the stairs.

Emmy rolled her eyes and opened her coloring book.

U talkg all boyz? Josie texted.

Just the 1s I kno!! I havnt met any here, thats 4 sure.

"You've had a visitor." Mom told me when I got home. She shifted the laundry hamper against her hip. "We had a nice chat. She knits!"

"Who knits?"

"Chloe."

"It's Cleo," I told her. "How do you know she knits?"

"I asked about her hat."

In the past week, I'd not yet seen Cleo bareheaded. Perhaps she was bald.

"I gave her your number," said Mom. "But she said she would drop by after supper."

I glanced at my phone, but the only message was from Selena. "I do have homework, you know," I said.

"Isn't it about time you made some friends?" said Mom.

"Cleo has piercings, Mother. In case you didn't notice. Probably tats. You know? Tattoos? Anyway, I have friends."

Though right now I had no patience for more of Selena's dance postmortem.

Mom dropped two piles of clothes on the bed. "Friends *here*, Daria. Not ones that you spend hours with on your phone."

"First you drag me away from Calgary. Now you won't let me talk to my friends?"

"You do exaggerate." Mom sat on the bed. "I simply said that you might make an effort to make friends here."

"And you think Cleo is a likely candidate?"

"Well, I will admit, she is a little…"

"Weird?"

"Don't be so judgmental," said Mom. "She certainly has her own style."

"She's in honors math, for Pete's sake. We have nothing in common."

"She seemed nice." Mom picked up the laundry basket. "But far be it from me to suggest who you should have for friends."

Far be it from you to run my life, I thought as she left the room. I stuffed the clean clothes in the nearest drawer.

All evening, I was alert for every passing car or knock at the front door.

I half imagined taking Cleo upstairs, showing her the dresser my grandfather had made. The pictures of the trip Josie and I took with the youth group last summer while Selena was at nature camp.

She didn't show up. By the time I went to bed, I was as annoyed as if I had been stood up. It was ridiculous. If I did make new friends here—not that I planned to—it would not be with a girl who wore homemade hats.

The next morning when I saw Cleo in the hallway, I expected her to stop. But she sailed by, waving at someone outside the cafeteria. Today her hat was pink with orange flowers around the brim.

I hugged my books to my chest, my phone in one hand and a can of apple juice in the other. I got a whiff of the juice. Caden was right. I ditched the can on the windowsill next to a wad of gum and a bus transfer.

Cleo flapped one hand in a feeble wave as I passed. But she kept talking to Drew Galling. Honors math student meets chess freak, I thought. A match made in heaven. Maybe she'd get off my back now.

Chapter Four

In class, I logged onto Facebook. When I couldn't think of an update to post, I scrolled through my text messages.

Hav u got my fav blu sweater? Selena asked.

Blu sweater? It was hanging in my closet at this very minute.

The 1 that goes with the gry skirt u pinched fr J.

"Who do you talk to all the time?" Cleo was unpacking her bag as carefully as always. "A boyfriend?"

"Shut up!" I said. "Just friends. From my old school."

Gry skirt? I texted. This could go on all day.

"You know it can be an addiction?" asked Cleo. "Social media. Email, texting, online searching, games," she recited. "Twitter. Facebook. All that stuff."

"Everyone does it," I told her as I typed in **Wear the green 1 u pinched fr me.** "Anyway," I said to Cleo, "how would you know? I've never seen you with a phone."

"Remember books?" she asked. "Newspapers and magazines? Internet addiction is all over them these days. Articles, studies and such." She fingered one of the flowers on her hat. "I know all about addictions."

There didn't seem to be a proper response to this. But I couldn't help asking anyway. "You do?"

"Not me. But my dad, he's an alcoholic," said Cleo. "Nine years dry, but still an alcoholic. He knows everything there is to know about addictions." She counted off her fingers. "Heroin. Gambling. Alcohol. Chocolate. Internet use." She looked at her hand. "There are tons more too. Shopping. Hand washing…"

"I am not addicted." The words were hardly out of my mouth when my phone beeped.

I made a face. Cleo laughed.

Okay, I laughed too. "Technology is important," I told her over the ringtone. "My dad says it levels the playing field. We all have access to the same information, thanks to technology. He works in the *Sun*'s printing plant. He knows all about technology. Now look what you've done. I've missed my call," I said.

"That's elitist," said Cleo.

"What's elitist? What do you mean?"

"It assumes that everyone has access," she said. "Poor people. The elderly. Homeless…"

There was no time to get into it with her. The English teacher strode through the door reciting, from a book. But she never looked at the page once. On and on she went, her eyes scanning the students as the words poured from her mouth.

How many poems could one person memorize?

The class soon settled and fell silent.

"Good. Thanks, everyone." Ms. Watson closed the book and put it on her desk. I held my phone on my lap to google a few words I recalled from the poem. Later, I would teach Cleo the importance of access to information by telling her who wrote the poem and when.

"That poem Ms. Watson was reciting? I checked online," I told Cleo after school. I held out my phone to show her the Wiki article. "It's by the same guy who wrote *The Just So Stories*. Did you read them when you were a kid?"

She didn't bother to check the screen. "Sure, I know Rudyard Kipling. The poem's called 'If.' Any fool knows that." She stopped in the middle of the sidewalk and put down her bag. When she shook back her hair, the purple tassel on top of her hat shivered. "If you can keep your head when all about you / Are losing theirs and blaming it on you," she recited. "If you can trust yourself when all men doubt you / But make allowance for their doubting too…"

It didn't take long for Cleo's performance and her weird getup to attract an audience. A guy in a hard hat and dusty work boots whistled. A woman wearing runners with her business suit looked up from her phone.

"Okay. I get the message."

Cleo ignored me. "If you can talk with crowds and keep your virtue / Or walk with kings, nor lose the common touch…"

#? poems do u know? I texted Selena.

WWTK? Twinkle Twinkle Little Star. The Hiwayman. Is this a test?

I loved "The Highwayman." But even between the two of us, we could never remember all the words. **More ltr. GTG** I texted her when I realized Cleo had finally wound down.

She picked up her bag and tugged her hat. "I should have passed this around to make a buck or two," she said as two women walked away smiling.

"Doesn't that ring in your lip hurt?" I asked.

"This?" As Cleo tugged on it, her lip stretched out, showing the moist skin inside.

I winced. "It hurts just to look at it."

"I forget it's there." Cleo slung her bag across her shoulder. A bunch of kids at the bus stop stared at us, muttering as we passed them.

"Don't your parents care?" I asked.

She pulled on her lip again and peered down at it cross-eyed. "When I was twelve, they told me that if they put no limits on me, I would set them myself." She grinned. "So I got pierced. And a tattoo, which I had to do myself. I'll show you sometime. Last Christmas, in our last house, I spent the day painting my room black and playing the Grateful Dead. Better than lentil loaf with the rellies any day."

"You can do anything you want?"

"It may sound like freedom," said Cleo. "But Mom and Dad still run the show. No red meat or smoking tobacco in the house. No aerosols. No TV."

"You're kidding!" The new flat-screen Dad bought when we moved took up a whole wall of the living room.

"It's no big deal," she said.

"You can download stuff, though, right?" I asked. "Movies? Documentaries, even? Music videos?"

"We don't have a computer."

"No computer?" What planet did this girl come from?

"But they know me well at the library." Cleo grinned. "The one here has fourteen computer stations. Back in Westbank, only three!"

"What about a phone?"

"Course I have a phone." Cleo grinned and slapped her forehead. "Silly me. You mean a cell phone, right? No."

No red meat was one thing. But no cell, or smartphone or iPad? "How do you keep in touch with people? With what's going on? How do your parents check up on you?"

"I'm supposed to be where I say I'm going to be. And be home when I say I'll be home. I had a bunch of buddies in Westbank. But the place was so small, we hardly ever needed to phone each other. It won't take me long to get connected here." Cleo grinned. "I already met you, didn't I?"

"Sounds so…I dunno," I said. "I could never live like that, disconnected from everything." I could have told her about the Cool Code of Conduct. But that was something between Selena and Josie and me.

"I guess it goes back to when my grandparents lived in a cabin on a creek with no running water, maybe," said Cleo.

How very *Little House on the Prairie*!

But Cleo's family story was fascinating, the way she told it. Her grandmother had been a potter. Her grandfather, a Vietnam War draft dodger. They had lived on a mountain, "off the grid." According to Cleo, this meant no running water or electricity, let alone phones or TV. Talk about disconnected! They grew all their own stuff. Self-sufficiency, Cleo called it. They passed their values on to Cleo's mother.

The way she told it, her family lived the kind of life I thought had died out about the time of Laura Ingalls Wilder.

My phone alarm buzzed. I grabbed Cleo's arm. "What's the time?"

"What's the panic?"

"The kids I babysit." I took off running. "I have to be there when they get home."

Chapter Five

Cleo was right beside me as I raced toward the intersection, past the library, through the park and across the street against the light.

When a driver pounded his horn and yelled "Stupid kids!" out the window, I just ran faster.

My breath was raw in my throat by the time we got to the house. A gray minivan idled at the sidewalk.

Caden pushed his way through the kids who were jammed in among coats and lunch boxes. "Where were you? We've been here for ages."

Emmy emerged holding a piece of poster board. "You're late." She pushed it into my hands. "I have to do a science project."

Today's driver was a thin woman with a gray-white sheet of hair. "I have an appointment, you know." She looked at her watch. "They will charge me if I don't make it in time."

"Sorry to hold you up," I said.

The woman was too busy nagging everyone to buckle up to answer. She slammed the doors, hurried around to the driver's side and drove off.

"Jacob's mom said lots of rude words when you weren't here," Emmy said as I groped for the key.

"Lots and lots," agreed Caden.

Cleo followed as I shepherded the

kids inside. "Do you know anything about science projects?" I asked her.

She hung up her jacket and placed her shoes against the wall. But she didn't take off her hat. "Sure. I won my school science fair."

How come I'm not surprised, I thought.

"Three times," she added as she followed us into the kitchen.

The kids didn't find anything odd about a total stranger opening cupboard doors and peering into the fridge.

After a snack, Caden whined that he wanted to do a science project of his own. Cleo distracted him by asking about his LEGO, and he happily trotted out of the room.

That was close, I texted Josie. **Late for work.**

U tk a babysitting course? she asked.

1st aid.

Not the same thing.

Im the 1 wth the job. Though it might be hard to tell right now, with Cleo taking charge.

She had stuck a sheet of paper on the fridge with four flower magnets. "All you need to do is answer the five Ws and one H," she told Emmy as she scrawled a big W across the paper.

Gotta go. Big science project, I texted Josie. If I wasn't careful, Cleo might ask me to split my pay with her.

U tkg science this semestr?

Explain later, I told her. **Call me.**

Emerson munched her cookie as Cleo continued. "What? Who? Where? When? Why? And How? First decide your topic," she told Emmy. "Then figure out your questions. Answer them, and you'll be done." I could hear footsteps and rattling toys overhead. Caden would be busy for a while.

I was ready to explain Cleo's research methods to Josie, but it wasn't her on the phone when it rang. "Where are you?" said Mom. No *Hello. How was your day?*

"Babysitting. It's Tuesday."

"Cynthia was worried. She called the house."

"When?"

"Just after two forty-five. No one answered."

"I was only a couple of minutes late."

"Only a couple of minutes?" My mother's voice was chilly.

"The car pool had just got here when we arrived." Trust her to make a big deal out of it.

"We? Is it okay to have people over when you're babysitting?"

"Cynthia never said."

"Who is there with you?"

"Cleo."

Cleo looked up when she heard her name.

"And who is Cleo?" Mom asked.

"You met her, remember? She knits."

Cleo tapped her hat and grinned.

"Why didn't Cynthia call again herself?" I asked Mom.

"She had to go into a meeting. I was to get her out of there if there was still no answer."

I could hear Caden yelling upstairs. "Look, I've got to go. I'll see you later."

"I'll tell Cynthia that everything's okay," said Mom. I could hear the smile in her voice when she added, "It's nice to know you've made a friend."

I hung up without saying goodbye. One minute, she's on my case because I'm two minutes late. Now, everything is forgiven because I have a friend!

"You going to help, or what?" asked Cleo. "Caden's calling you."

"He'll be fine for a minute," I said as I checked my messages.

Im in the festivl!!! Jazz & tap!!! Selena had texted.

Deets ltr? I answered. **Im @ wrk!!!**

"Cleo is going to show me how to make a tin-can phone," said Emmy. "Have we got any cans?"

I pushed the blue box toward them with my foot. "Isn't Emmy too young to get addicted to phones?" I said to Cleo.

"Idiot!" Cleo said as she dug in the box for some cans.

When my phone rang, she leaned across and grabbed it. She peered at the screen. "One of your buddies, looks like. Leave it, can't you? We've got a science project to do."

Chapter Six

By the time I called her back after I got home, Josie had left one message and Selena two.

"That's great about the festival," I told Selena as she picked up.

She cut me off. "Yeah. It is. But that not why I called."

"Bet you're pleased though. I know you were ticked about the bronze—"

She interrupted, talking fast. "Look, Daria. It's about our trip. There's been a change of plans. It turns out Dad's car needs…well, something real expensive. And see, there's only room for three in the back of Mom's Kia."

"We've done it before. Lots of times."

"Yeah. But not as far as Quebec. With all our stuff."

"So?"

I could hear her swallow.

"What?" I asked.

"It's not like it's the only chance we'll have. Next year, I'll make sure…"

"Selena, what are you telling me?"

Her words came out in a rush. "There won't be room for you. Not this time. Not with me and Justine and Josie."

"Justine?" I pulled my pillow into my lap. I hugged it. "Justine Marcus is going with you?"

"You know her mom knows my mom? They were talking and before I knew it…"

"Justine?"

"Stop saying it like that. Like I said, there's only room for three of us. Mom and Dad in the front…"

"I know how many seats there are in your mom's damn car. I've been in it often enough." The three of us in the back. Sharing magazines. Doing our nails. Playing Scrabble. "We've been planning this for ages," I said. "You, me and Josie. Like always. Now you want to take Justine instead?"

"Not really. But when her mom…"

"Right. Of course. It's not your fault. It's her mom's. Your mom's. You know what?" I held the phone away at arm's length. I took a deep breath, then put it back to my ear. "Sure. Go ahead," I said. "Fine. You and Josie have a good time with Justine. I have better things to do with my hard-earned money than spend it all on a holiday with you…you jerks." I hung up before she could say another word.

I swiped at the tears and leaned back against the wall. I stared at the screen, willing Selena to call back, to text me. While I waited, I ran through all the mean and awful things I would say to her.

The phone did not ring. The screen stayed blank.

I shoved my pillow back under my head and jammed the phone underneath.

When Mom called me for supper, I yelled that I didn't want any. When she knocked on my door later, I pressed my face into the pillow so she wouldn't hear me crying.

I pulled out my phone and punched in a whole bunch of texts to Josie.

That cow Selena!

Remember the CCC? #3? Stick together?

U kno that gry skirt? I do hav it. It's perfect wth the blu shirt!

I hate this. Call me.

BFF my ass.

Dont u dare try 2 make xcuses.

I deleted them all.

I turned my phone off and threw it across the room. When it fell behind my chair, I didn't bother to check it was okay.

I crawled into bed, pulled the covers up to my head.

Mom and Dad knocked during the evening. When I didn't answer, they whispered to each other and then went away.

Next morning, my phone worked. But there was nothing from Selena. Or Josie.

All the way to school, I worked on what I would say to them. If we ever spoke again.

By lunch, they had still not called or texted me. "Want to see a movie on the weekend?" I asked Cleo at lunch.

"Sure you've got time for me between keeping in touch with old friends and babysitting?" She peered inside her wrap, then rolled it back up.

"You said you liked movies."

"I thought you were saving all your pay for your trip to Calgary?"

"I'm not going."

"How come?" Cleo asked.

"Josie and Selena are taking this dumb girl they hardly know. Justine," I sneered. "Justine Marcus. It's not like she's a friend or anything. She just stands next to them in the choir." I would have told Cleo that used to be my spot, but I didn't want to start crying again.

"So did you have a big bust-up when they told you?"

"Kind of. I guess so." I never wanted to speak to Selena again. Josie neither. She could have voted Justine out of the trip and insisted I came along. She should have. But she didn't.

Cleo eyed my fries. "I had this friend in Westbank, Lauren, since kindergarten. In grade seven she came with us on a road trip into the Rockies. In exchange,

I was supposed to go to Disneyland with her family. Somewhere my parents would never go."

"You haven't been to Disneyland?" I asked her.

Cleo flapped a hand as if that wasn't what mattered. "The point is, when they finally went, they said they wanted a family trip. So they took a cousin Lauren had never even met."

"Ouch."

Cleo flipped her hat strings. "When they got back, they were buddies. The cousin was in, and I was out." She grabbed a fry. "Your friends are dumb if they don't invite you to go with them."

"Well..." I wanted to defend Josie and Selena. Rule number three in the Cool Code was Stick Together.

Though why should I care? I'd been gone less than two months, and I'd already been replaced.

"It's like little kids on a playground," said Cleo. "I can't be friends with you because you are friends with someone I'm not friends with," she went on in a singsong voice. "Like there's not enough friendship to go around." When she flung her arms out, a guy carrying a loaded tray nearly dumped it on the giggling girls at the next table. "There's enough love in the world for everyone," Cleo announced.

Was it them she was talking about? Or me?

I got busy plucking sprouts out of my sandwich.

Cleo laughed. "That's how my parents talk." She grabbed a fry from my plate. "You don't have to worry about that lot and their fancy holiday in *la belle* Quebec. You've got me!"

I took a long drink of pop. "You want the rest of these?" I shoved my plate toward her.

As we headed out of the cafeteria, Cleo asked, "How's Emmy doing with her science project?"

"She wants me to help her decorate the tin cans tonight."

"One of my collages hung in the hallway at Westbank Central for a whole term."

Of course it did. As soon as I caught the mean thought, I said, "So, Van Gogh. You want to come over and help?"

She grinned and put her arm through mine. "Sure."

"Great. Do you need to let your mom know you won't be home right away?"

"Shoot." Cleo slapped her forehead dramatically. "I have to help her assemble her new loom. Tomorrow, though? I've got loads of cool craft stuff at my house I can bring over."

"Okay."

"What about that movie?" she asked. "Shall I check the papers to see what's on?"

I thought we would download something to watch at my place. I could impress her with our new huge flatscreen. But she'd probably just tell me about growing up watching magic lantern shows, or whatever they use on *Little House on the Prairie*. "Tell you what," I said. "Let's talk tonight, and we can figure out what to do."

"Sounds good," said Cleo. "Give the kids a hug from me. Especially that sweetie pie Cade."

Chapter Seven

My phone kept getting buried under Emmy's craft stuff spread across the kitchen table.

"Will you come and play with my space station?" Caden asked me. A milk mustache was smeared across his face.

"In a bit," I told him. I picked up my phone. Maybe if I logged on to the movie listings, Josie or Selena would call.

"Okay. But hurry up." He dashed out of the room.

Emmy was busy cutting paper, her tongue poking out between her teeth. I had run through all the local movie listings by the time Caden yelled down.

"I'll be right up," I answered. I checked to see if Josie and Selena had posted anything on Facebook.

Caden yelled something else I couldn't understand.

"Daria!" Emmy looked over at me and rolled her eyes. Then she continued cutting.

A text beeped. Josie. **U still talking to me? Us? Call me. Now. Im home. Call me. OK? PP.**

"I'm going into the living room," I told Emmy.

"Caden wants you," she said. "Can't you hear him?"

"I'll go up in a minute."

I was settling onto the couch when I heard thumps overhead. What on earth was the kid doing now? Rearranging the furniture? My phone beeped again. I thought I never wanted to speak to Selena again. But what had Cleo said? *There's always enough friendship to go around.*

"Hi," is all I said. I didn't plan to make this easy.

"I know you're mad at us," Josie said. "I don't blame you. Honest, Dari. It wasn't my idea…"

"You could have stood up for me."

"I tried. But I swear. It was Selena's mom. We didn't stand a chance once she suggested it to Justine's mom."

"I can't believe—"

"I know. She'll wreck the whole trip. You know Justine's allergic to almost everything, right? And you know what? She's bilingual, she says. I bet she's going to practice all the way to Quebec."

I held my hand against one ear to shut out the noise from upstairs. *"Comment allez-vous?"* I said in my clunkiest accent. "*Voulez-vous danser avec moi?*"

Josie laughed. "*Mais oui, monsieur.* But I guess it might be useful having someone who speaks it," she said.

"If you say so."

"I didn't mean it like that. Honest, Daria. I hate that you're not coming with us. Hey, did I tell you about this great shirt I bought at Mexx last week?" And suddenly it was as if we were in the same room instead of separated by a thousand kilometers and a bunch of mountains.

As I lay back with my feet on the arm of the couch, the door flew open. "Go away, Emmy." I held the phone against my chest. "I won't be long."

She charged at me. "You've got to come. Caden is hurt." She grabbed my arm.

"Just a minute." I tried to shake free.

Her hard little fingers dug into me. "Caden's hurt," she shrieked. "There's blood all over the floor. He won't get up. You've got to come!"

I threw down my phone and raced after Emmy. I overtook her halfway up the stairs and charged into Caden's room.

It was empty.

"He's in Mom and Dad's room," Emmy screeched.

Caden lay on the floor between the bed and the dresser. One arm was flung above his head. The other was twisted underneath his body. His face was white, his eyes closed. Around his head was a pool of sticky dark blood.

Emmy dropped down beside him. "Cady. Wake up." She patted his face. His eyelids quivered, but he did not open his eyes.

"Don't touch him," I yelled. What had they taught us in First Aid? Something about pressing on the wound. But where was it?

Then I remembered another instruction. Don't move the patient.

But I couldn't leave him there. I hooked my arm under his shoulders and pulled him across my lap. I felt wetness smearing along my arm.

"Is he dead?" stammered Emmy.

"Of course he isn't," I said. But how could I tell? He was so still and pale. "We have to call an ambulance. Get my phone."

"I want Mommy." Emmy's sobs grew louder. "Caden is going to die, isn't he?"

"Stop saying that!" I could hear the panic in my voice. "We have to call nine-one-one."

She sat back on her heels, hugging herself. "I want Mommy."

Caden lay like a dead weight in my lap. "Emmy." I struggled to keep my voice low and level to make her do as she was told without frightening her. "You have to call nine-one-one.

It's very important. Or get me the phone.
You have to do it right now. Do you
hear me?"

"Okay." She was shaking. Her eyes
were blank.

"Get up now. Go downstairs. Bring
me my phone."

Emmy looked around.

"Emerson!" I couldn't keep the panic
out of my voice.

She stood up and turned around.

"It's downstairs," I said. "Call nine-
one-one. Do you know your address?"

"9631 Lakeview Crescent, Delta, BC,
Canada." Emmy spoke slowly as if she
was memorizing it. "9631…"

"Emmy! Get my phone," I yelled.
"Now!"

"There's one here." She picked it up
from the table under the window.

I took a deep breath. "Dial nine-one-
one. Can you do that?"

"We learned that in Brownies."

"That's great." I tried to keep my voice normal, even though my heart pounded in my chest like a hammer. "Now dial. Tell them where we are. Then hold the phone up to my ear so I can hear what they say."

Emerson prodded the keypad. She pressed the phone to her own ear for a moment before she held it toward me. "Do we need the police or the ambulance?"

"Ambulance!" The pool of blood seeping into the carpet seemed bigger and darker.

"Ambulance, please." Now Emerson spoke as coolly as if she was asking for a peanut-butter sandwich. She repeated the address twice. Then she leaned across Caden and held the phone toward me.

It took all of my self-control to answer the dispatcher's questions. To repeat everything twice. Admitting that yes, I had moved Caden. That he was not conscious. But that I could feel him breathing. "There's blood," I said. "Lots of it." My voice was shaking.

Emerson was huddled on the floor next to me. Tears streamed down her face. Her red and swollen eyes did not leave my face.

"No, I don't know where it's coming from," I said into the phone.

"Stay on the line with me," said the dispatcher. "Can you do that? Emergency Services will be there in about six minutes."

"Hurry. Please."

"Don't hang up. Can you put a blanket over the little boy?"

I eased one hand from under Caden and dragged the quilt off the bed behind me. I draped it over him and across my own shoulder. Emmy tucked herself against my side.

Six minutes had never seemed so long. I held Caden while his sister's sobs vibrated against my arm. I should comfort her. But all I could think of was the little boy in my arms and the blood soaking my sleeve and spreading around us.

The dispatcher suddenly said, "Daria. They're at the house now. Is the door open?"

I could hear sirens on the street. Then banging downstairs.

"It's them!" Emerson dashed out of the room.

"Hello!" Voices from the front hall were followed by heavy footsteps on the stairs. "It's the paramedics."

"Everything's fine," I whispered to Caden. "You'll be fine now."

It sounded good. Even if I did not believe it.

Chapter Eight

Emmy wandered around the waiting room. She checked out posters and studied the signs at the admissions desk. She watched a pair of paramedics wheel an empty gurney outside.

"Come here." Even wrapped in a blanket, I could not stop shivering. "Emerson. Stay with me."

"Will Caden be better soon?" She leaned against my leg. "Where's Mommy?"

"She'll be here." The paramedics had called Cynthia from the cold, stark ambulance. Shining equipment hung above Caden as he had lain still and silent under the covers, his head almost completely covered in a gauze pad.

"Here's Mom!" Emerson rushed into Cynthia's arms. She burst into tears. "Cady got hurt," she sobbed. "There was blood everywhere."

"It's okay, Em." Her mother stroked her back. "Let's go see him, shall we?" When I stood up to go with them, she said, " You stay here. We need to see what the doctor has to say."

They disappeared through the swinging doors.

I huddled inside the blanket, desperate for someone to talk to. Anyone. Anything to distract me from wondering how long Caden might be unconscious. If he had brain damage. How he had ended up lying in a pool of blood.

I looked around, then remembered that my backpack was still at the kids' house. So was my phone. If I ever needed to talk to someone, it was now.

As I picked up an old *Us* magazine, the doors wheezed open, letting in a gust of cold air. My mother rushed toward me.

As soon as I stood up, I started to cry.

Mom hugged me quickly, then eased me into a chair. She pulled another one close and sat down. "I drove Cynthia. I had to park across the street." She pushed a strand of hair away from my cheek. "Want to tell me what happened?"

"I don't know." I took a deep breath. "He was upstairs playing while I was downstairs with Emmy. She must have heard Caden fall." The image of his pallid face rose in front of me. "There was so much blood…"

"Head wounds are often like that," Mom said. "Is Emmy with her mother?"

"They went to see the doctor," I gulped.

"Let's wait, then." She held my hand as she looked across at a woman in a bright purple sari holding a sleeping baby. A girl my age cracked gum as she read a magazine. Two little boys chased each other around an empty wheelchair.

One announcement after another came over the PA. Paging a doctor whose name I couldn't make out. Telling another to report to radiology. Asking for an admissions nurse. Phones rang. Doors opened and closed. The sound of footsteps and voices, moving trolleys and clattering equipment seeped out from the treatment rooms. Ambulances wailed in the distance.

After what seemed hours, the door opened. Emerson darted through. "Hi, Daria's mom," she said. "Caden woke up.

He's mad that I got to ride in the front with the driver and he didn't." She plonked down on the empty chair beside Mom. "His arm was in the wrong place. They yanked it back the right way. He's going to get stitches. I bet we'll hear him yell from here." She bounced on her seat. "Can I have some chips?"

Mom dug into her purse and gave her some coins. "Go ahead."

"I can't reach the buttons."

"I'll help you." I stepped out of the blanket, glad to have something to do.

"I want your mom to do it," said Emmy as she grabbed Mom's hand. "Not you."

Emerson had eaten her chips and drunk a can of apple juice by the time her mother came out.

"He's conscious. He tried to be brave." Cynthia's eyes filled with tears. "But that's a lot of stitches for a little boy."

"How many?" asked Emerson.

"Twenty-one."

Mom stood up and hugged Cynthia. "How bad is it?"

"He has a mild concussion. But it's probably not as bad as it looks." Cynthia watched Emerson playing peek-a-boo with the baby on the woman's lap. "He had been bouncing on my bed, he told me. Even though he knows he's not allowed in my room." She glanced at me, then back toward the treatment rooms. "They want to keep him overnight. I'm going home to get some things. I wonder, if it's not too much to ask…?"

"Emerson can stay with us," said Mom. "Daria will be happy to help, won't you, love?"

"I'd prefer that you watched Emmy," said Cynthia.

"Why? What's wrong?" asked Mom.

"I asked Emerson why Caden was in my room," said Cynthia. "Where Daria was when he was jumping on the bed."

"Daria was downstairs with Emmy." Mom frowned at me. "Isn't that what you said?"

I studied the scuff marks on the floor.

"Emmy was in the kitchen working on her science project." Cynthia's voice was cold. "Daria was in the living room. On her phone. She ignored Caden calling her. And she did not hear him fall. Emmy was the one to find him unconscious on the floor. His seven-year-old sister."

I felt a flush spread up my face as Mom, Cynthia and Emerson stared at me.

Chapter Nine

On the way home, I was aware of every sound. Mom's breathing. The road noise under the tires. A hiss of wind through a crack in the back window. I wanted to speak. But I did not know what to tell her. I willed Mom to talk to me. But I was afraid of what she would say.

All she had said since we left the hospital was, "Buckle up."

When we pulled into the driveway, Mom reached for the door handle. But instead of opening it, she sat back and closed her eyes. "That little boy could have died."

"They said the wound was superficial."

She gave me such a cold look, I shrank away from her.

"It was *your* job to take care of those children," she said. "But you were too busy, what? Calling your friends? Texting? Emailing?" Her voice rose with every word. "Watching some damn thing on YouTube?" She closed her eyes again and tipped back her head.

"It was only for a minute or two."

"That is all it takes."

I swiped at the tears that trailed down my cheeks. "I am so sorry. But Caden is going to be all right. They said so. It was just a superficial wound." My mouth was running on even though my mind was telling me to shut it. "You know little boys. They fall off things all the time." I looked through a smear of tears at my father moving around indoors. "It's not my fault that Caden went into his mother's bedroom, is it?"

Mom's turned to glare at me. "You didn't see his mother's face when she got that call from the paramedics."

She slammed the car door and walked into the house.

The cooling metal of the car ticked under the hood.

I turned to grab my backpack from the backseat. Then I remembered it was still at the kids' house. And my phone was on the floor where I had dropped it when I dashed upstairs.

I dragged myself into the house.

When she dropped Emerson off later, Cynthia hardly looked at me. Mom gave Emmy a bowl of soup and tucked her in on the study futon.

I wanted to creep under my covers. But I didn't want to be alone. So I stayed downstairs, hardly speaking while Mom told Dad the whole story. Mom finally pushed her plate aside. She had barely eaten anything. Dad dumped his salad back in the bowl. "So no phone for a month," he said.

"That's so not fair," I said. "What if you need to reach me?" I stabbed my fork into a lettuce leaf and held it up. "What about Selena and Josie? I need to keep in touch with them. Since you dragged me here, they are the only friends I've got."

"And whose choice is that?" asked Mom. "Anyway, I thought you and Chloe were friends now?"

"It's Cleo!" When I shoved the table, my cutlery jumped. "How many times do I have to tell you?"

Dad gathered the dishes. "Your mother and I are not going to change our minds, Daria. I doubt very much you were talking to your friends for only a few minutes." When I opened my mouth to speak, he held up his hand. "Mom is concerned. I am too. We've let it slide for too long. But now it's a real problem."

"Let what slide? What are you talking about?"

"Your dependence on your phone. What amounts to an addiction. Do you know how little time you actually spend speaking to us, face-to-face? You would rather be texting your friends or watching those damn YouTube videos than spending time with your own parents."

Addiction? I had heard that somewhere recently. "That is such crap!" Dad winced, so I said it again, louder. "Crap," I said. "I talk to you. I watch TV."

"It's more than that, Daria. Everything you do or say or engage in is filtered through that damn phone."

"You bought it for me."

"That's not the point," he said, his voice rising. He ran his hand through his hair.

"So what is the point?" I asked.

"You always seem to be somewhere else. Instead of here." His hand slapped the table. "With the people around you. With whatever is going on. It's as if every text or call or Facebook posting is more important than what's happening here and now."

"That's so not true!"

"Isn't it?" Dad stood up. "Not only were you not in the room with the children you were babysitting. You weren't even in the house."

"I was so!"

"Perhaps you were there in body," Mom chimed in. "But your mind? It wasn't anywhere near that little boy when he hurt himself." She leaned so close, I could feel her breath. "You might as well have been in Timbuktu for all the help you were to that child."

Chapter Ten

All night, the covers kept bunching up. One minute, my room was too hot, then too cold. Every sound was louder than usual—the creak of my parents' door as they finally went to bed, the fridge cutting in and out. Every few minutes, I stuck my hand out, forgetting that my phone was not in its usual place next to my bed. The green numbers on my clock took forever to change.

The night lasted a lifetime.

Next morning, I dragged myself down to breakfast. I shoveled six spoonfuls of sugar onto my cereal. Mom watched me without saying a word. I ignored the phony bright conversation that Dad had going with Emerson.

She ignored me.

I had just got up from the table when Mom said, "You can go over and pick up your phone after school. But can I trust you not to use it?" She didn't wait for an answer. "Put it in Dad's desk. You can use the landline to let Selena and Josie know that your phone privileges are suspended. Email too." Then, as an afterthought, she added, "And anyone else who needs to know."

Phone. And email! "But even if I can't use my cell, I can still use the landline, right? And the desktop computer?"

"Weren't you listening last night?" Mom asked. "For homework only.

Not socializing. Do I need to go over it all again?"

I stomped upstairs. I locked myself in the bathroom and scrubbed my teeth so hard, I thought my gums would bleed. I swabbed my face with the towel, slapped on some makeup and headed out of the house without saying goodbye.

At school, when I saw Cleo coming my way, I ducked into the music room.

In math, the teacher kept telling me to stop flicking my pen against the desk. In Spanish, my hand kept straying to my pocket, then coming up empty. I was glad when lunch break finally arrived.

Cleo caught up with me in the cafeteria. "We still on for tonight?"

"Tonight what?"

"I was going to hang out with you. And Emmy and Cade…" She peered at me. "What's up?"

I looked into the distance, trying to blink away tears.

"You okay?" Cleo asked.

I blew my nose. "It's nothing. Must be my allergies."

"Allergies?"

I squeezed the damp tissue in my fist. "Not really."

"Let's go in here." Cleo hauled me into the washroom. She pulled me into the handicapped stall. "Tell me everything."

"Mom and Dad confiscated my phone," I told her. "For a whole month."

"I thought it was something serious. Brain cancer. One of your parents fired. Something really serious."

"It is serious."

"Well, okay. I can see it, I guess. But I thought you weren't talking to your best buddies since the bust-up about the spring-break trip."

"We made up, actually. If you must know." I glared at her.

"So why have you lost your phone privileges?"

"Dad says I'm addicted."

Cleo nodded. "He's been reading about it too, eh?"

Of course! It was Cleo who had thrown around the word *addiction*. As if I was a junkie. Or gambled away my allowance.

"So that's all?" she asked. "You're crying because you can't use your phone for a while?" She slid down the wall until she was sitting on her bag. She leaped up again when someone banged on the door. "What?" she yelled. "We're busy in here."

"Do you mind?" a voice called from the other side.

"Who's that?" she hissed. "A teacher?"

"It's Whitney Houlden." I opened the door, and we left the stall to let Whitney ease her wheelchair in.

"Let's go to Timmy's for a coffee," said Cleo.

"It's not just because Dad says I'm addicted," I told her as I followed her outside. "Or dependent or whatever."

"What then?"

We dashed across the street and headed for the coffee shop. "Caden hurt himself yesterday," I said.

"He okay?" Cleo pulled a handful of coins from her pocket.

"He had to have twenty-one stitches."

"Twenty-one!" exclaimed Cleo. "What happened?"

Suddenly I felt very tired. "Let's get our drinks first."

When we were settled at a table, I told Cleo about finding Caden unconscious and the long wait for the ambulance. About the scene at the hospital when the kids' mother told Mom she didn't want me left alone with Emerson.

Cleo rested her chin on her hand. Her eyes hardly left my face as talked. I told her everything, even about the blood. Caden so still and pale. Everything.

The whole time we talked, my hand kept drifting toward my pocket, then back to the table. I shook a sugar packet until the sugar settled at one end, then the other. Was this how smokers feel, I wondered, when they try to quit? Twitchy. Nervous. Spaced out.

"I'm only allowed to use the computer at home for homework," I told her. "And I've probably lost my job too. Now I'll never get back to Calgary." I tore the sugar packet into tiny pieces and piled them into a little heap. "Everything is the pits." A tear splashed on the table.

"That's a bummer," Cleo agreed. "But I'm sure Caden will be fine. He's a tough little guy. And hey!" She grinned at me. "We can hang out more. Now you don't have to babysit. And without your phone or email, you'll need someone to talk to." She poked herself in the chest.

"And here I am!" She sat back, looking pleased with herself.

"I feel so…kind of…" I groped for the word. "Not abandoned. Adrift," I said. "Like I'm stuck out here, out of touch with everything that's going on."

I could tell by her face that she couldn't connect with what I was saying.

Suddenly I was aware of how hot the restaurant was. It was noisy with clattering dishes and loud voices, ringing phones and the crash of the cash register.

I felt trapped. Penned in. "I'm out of here." I drained my drink and crumpled the cup. "I'm heading home."

Cleo glanced at the wall clock. "What about social studies? Stryker's setting the big assignment today."

"Forget socials." I dropped my cup into the garbage. "Who cares about a dumb assignment."

I was running as soon as I was through the door.

Chapter Eleven

As soon as I got home, I realized I should have gone to the kids' house first to get my stuff.

I went downstairs to the den. I shed my jacket as I waited for Dad's old PC to power up. I found nine emails from Selena. Four from Josie. And they'd posted frantic messages on Facebook too, using caps. *WHERE ARE YOU? EARTH TO D!*

I was still mad. With Selena especially. But I was so used to telling them everything. I started an email to explain what was going on. But it sounded lame. Then melodramatic and whiny. I rewrote it, deleted that, then started again.

I checked the clock on the corner of the screen. They would be at one of their houses. Or at the Little Chef Café.

I deleted the last message without sending it, grabbed the phone from the kitchen and headed upstairs.

I dropped onto my bed and adjusted the pillows with one hand as I dialed with the other. I might as well be comfortable if this was to be the last time I ever got to talk to them.

As soon as Josie answered, I told her about having my phone confiscated.

I kept my voice low, even though I knew it would be ages before Mom got home.

Josie and Selena passed the phone back and forth between them. "Are you kidding?" "That can't be right." "That's child cruelty." "They can't do that!"

At last they left enough breathing space for me to tell them why Mom and Dad had confiscated my phone. And why I wasn't allowed to email. "It's because one of the kids I was babysitting had an accident while I was on the phone. That's why I couldn't call Josie back yesterday," I said.

"Daria," said Selena. "I'm mad at my mom, you know. It's all…"

"Forget it. It doesn't matter," I told her. It seemed so unimportant, compared to the memory of Caden, dead-white, not moving, with a pool of blood under his head.

But I didn't tell them about the blood. I didn't tell them about the hospital. And I didn't tell them what Dad had said. About me not being there with the kids while I was on the phone.

Until now, Selena, Josie and I had always told each other everything.

I turned toward the clock radio on my bedside table. "I've got to go," I said. "I'll catch it if they hear me on the phone."

"So we really can't reach you for a month?" asked Selena.

"That is SO brutal," said Josie.

"I'll try to connect with you later." Maybe I could squeeze in a call or two after I'd picked up my phone from the kids' house.

In the kitchen, I replaced the phone on its base and grabbed a snack. As I opened a can of juice, I thought of Caden running around the house yelling "Vomitvomitvomit" and giggling like a maniac. I longed to hug his wiry little body and nuzzle his neck to make him laugh. So I went downstairs, grabbed my jacket and headed out again.

Emmy opened the door, swinging her homemade phone by its string.

"Mommy!" she called behind her. "Daria is here." She frowned at me. "My mom is real mad with you. We have to find another sitter."

Caden pushed in front of her. "I had to stay in the hospital," he said. "I got shaved and they gave me twenty-one stitches in my head." When he turned around, I could see a white bandage taped across his scalp.

Ms. Clarkson appeared behind him. "I thought I told you not to run around." She put a hand on Caden's shoulder and looked at me without smiling. "I expect you are here for your backpack."

"And my phone."

"You'd better come in." Ms. Clarkson stepped aside to let me pass.

"I nearly bleeded to death," Caden boasted as we headed for the kitchen. "The ambulance people saved my life. I was asleep," he told me. "If I had been awake, I could have drived in the front with Emmy."

"Don't keep telling it over and over," said Emerson.

Caden ignored her. "I had lots of stitches. It hurt so much. But I was very brave. Right, Mom?"

"You were very brave." His mother smiled at him. "Now, how about you and your sister go and play?

"But I want to show Daria my new LEGO," whined Caden. "It's a fire truck!" he told me.

"Do as you're asked." Ms. Clarkson steered the kids out of the room.

"I just came for my things," I said.

She handed me my backpack. "It's all here."

I itched to find the phone and stuff it in my pocket, where it belonged. Instead, I wrapped my arms around my bag. "I really am sorry about Caden's fall."

"I expect you are." I felt a flash of hope until she added, "But I trusted you to take care of my children." She blinked away tears. "We're just lucky it wasn't much worse."

"Can I say goodbye to the kids?" I asked quickly before I started crying.

"Of course. Take care of yourself, Daria."

I could feel her watching as I ducked into the living room. "Bye, guys," I said. "I've got to go now."

Caden was lying on his stomach on the floor stacking LEGO blocks. "Bye," he called without looking up.

"I finished my project," Emerson told me. "I wanted to show your friend."

"Maybe another time."

I stumbled out of the house and down the front path without looking back.

Chapter Twelve

The next day, Cleo dragged me into the
library on our way home from school.
She settled in front of a computer.
"I hope I can find this stuff again. I told
you. There's loads about technology
addiction." She clicked on one article after
another. "See?" she said. "Discomfort.
Short temper. Anxiety. That's you."

"I don't have a short temper," I snapped.

"It says here that it's much like any other addiction," said Cleo. "It shares many of the same withdrawal symptoms. It's an illness, really. And you're not the only one." She glanced around the library. Some people were reading in the lounge chairs. Others were hunched over tables, studying. But nearly everyone had a phone sitting beside them, was plugged into an iPod or was texting. "Don't you think it would be a great topic for our socials report?" she asked.

"I thought you told Stryker we were going to do our project on homelessness?"

"That was the first thing that came into my head when she assigned us to work together. Do you have a better idea?"

"Not this, that's for sure." All I needed was to treat my rotten life like a research project. "What's wrong with homelessness?" I asked.

"Lots!"

"I mean for a project, you jerk."

"See. There you go again," said Cleo. "Temper, temper!" The purple pompom on her hat bobbed. "Do you happen to know any homeless people?" she asked. "If we do addictions, it would be like a real scientific study. I'll be the control, as I'm not addicted to anything. You could be the subject, seeing as you are the one who's hooked."

"Why me? What about your dad?"

"I'm talking about technology here. Not booze. So shall we do this or not?"

"All right, all right," I said. Wet rag meets bulldozer, I thought. I knew which one I was. "But before we get into it, let me check Facebook while I have the chance."

"This can be the first experiment." Cleo grabbed the mouse as I tried to move the cursor to the address bar. "We need to document what happens when you are prevented from feeding your addiction."

"Give that to me." I tried to yank the mouse back.

She held on tight. "Withdrawal symptom number one. Impatience."

"Cleo!" I squeezed her hand.

"Violence now? I'd better record this stuff." When she released the mouse to reach for her bag, I grabbed it.

She hauled it away from me by its cord.

"Girls. Girls. You know the rule. One person at a work station at a time," said the librarian with the red spiky hair. "If you can't work quietly, I'll suspend your Internet privileges for the day."

"Excuse my friend," Cleo told her. "She's going through withdrawal. But we're cool."

"Thanks a lot," I hissed as the librarian went back to her desk.

"Loss of sense of humor. Must include that in our observations. This is going to be great!" Cleo picked up her bag and stood up. "You log off, and I'll find us a table."

"I'll be right there." I was about to open my email when I noticed one of the links. *Project Disconnect*, it said. I opened it up to find it was a website about a school in the United States that had banned all phones, iPods, iPads and other devices for a month.

"It would never catch on at our school," said Cleo. "Log on. Log off. Check this. Text that." She rolled her eyes. "One person in withdrawal at a time is all I can handle." She opened her binder and wrote down a bunch of notes. "Your task is to start a journal of all your symptoms. Make a note every time you feel the urge to connect with someone, and record the side effects of staying offline."

Any minute, I thought, she would stick me on a treadmill or clip wires to my head!

I'd often worked with Josie and Selena on projects. Josie was the one to assign tasks and set timelines. Then something would come up. Flu. A dance exam. Visitors from out of town. And soon Selena and I were on our own.

Cleo was a born organizer. And bossy too. By the time we left the library, we each had a list of things to do. Timelines, even.

She said she wanted an A for our first joint project.

And she didn't care what it took.

Chapter Thirteen

"How come you didn't call before?" said Selena when I snuck in a call before Mom got home.

"I told you. I'm not even supposed to use the phone. And I got hung up on this socials project at the library with Cleo."

"Who's Cleo?"

"Just some girl."

"What's she like?" There was an edge in her voice.

"She's okay. A bit weird, I guess."

"Weird, how?"

"I don't know. Just different." I could have told her about Cleo's hats and piercings and strange home life. But it felt disloyal. "Is Josie there?" I asked. "Let me talk to her. I don't know when I can connect again."

"She and Luca took off to check out some skateboards."

"Are they going out?" I asked.

"Ye-es! Like for at least two weeks! You really are out of the loop."

In the background, someone yelled for her to hurry up. "So what else is new?" I asked. "Selena?"

She was talking to someone else, away from the phone. Katya Blewett, I figured from the voice. "Selena?"

"Talk later, okay?" she said. "I've got to go."

I looked at the dead phone in my hand.

I dumped it on the floor and pulled my covers over my head. I might have gone to sleep if Mom hadn't stuck her head around the door. "Hi. Everything okay?"

I hadn't heard her come in. I swung my legs down, kicking the phone under the bed. "Fine."

"How was school?"

"Fine."

Mom shrugged. "Now we've had our mandatory hello-how-are-you conversation, I'll be in the kitchen."

I waited to hear that she was downstairs before I grabbed the phone and dialed Cleo's number.

"Hi. It's me. Daria."

"I could be your sponsor," she said. "Like in AA? Dad had one. Now he sponsors other people. When they feel tempted to drink, they call, and he talks them through it. Though I guess in your case, being as you are a recovering techno-phile, you are not likely to call for help on the very instrument you're with-drawing from. You think?"

I had to laugh. Cleo may be weird, but she was smart and funny.

"So what's up?" she asked.

"I thought I'd give you a call," I said. "I had to sneak the phone from downstairs. Now I have to figure out how to get it back without Mom seeing."

"Is that why we're whispering?" she whispered.

I told her about Josie and Luca. And Katya Blewett. Someone Selena had no time for before. Now they were hanging out together at the mall. I bet they could find room for *her* in Selena's mom's Kia.

"Well, people do move on, don't they?" said Cleo. "I've left people behind each time we moved. You can't stay friends forever with everyone you leave behind."

"What about that 'enough love to go around' stuff you were on about?" I asked.

"That's a load of crap." She laughed. "Well, not really. But you've got me now. Selena has Justine. Josie has Luca. It all works out. So, of all the guys in school, who do you have your eye on?"

She was trying so hard, and I was sick of talking about Selena and Josie. And Daria makes three. "You mean here?" I asked.

"Of course here. Me, myself and I? I think Drew Galling has a nice face."

"The chess freak?" I laughed. "You like his face? What about his arms? Or his shoulders or his chest?" I had never looked closely at any of them myself. "I'll have to think about it," I told her. "I'd better go before Mom sneaks up on me again."

"Me too. How are you feeling, by the way? Remember to keep notes of all your symptoms."

"Yeah, yeah. I'll do it as soon as I hang up." Which I thought was pretty funny.

The phone was safely under my pillow when Mom put her head around the door again. "Dad's home. Can you help with supper?"

The look she gave me reminded me of when I was at Nana's a few weeks ago, on the phone to Josie. "Do you remember when we used to cook together?" Nana had asked. That made me think of the woman at the mall telling me about her grandsons always texting.

What was it Dad said? I wondered. Something about not being in the same room?

"Sure. I can help," I said. I followed her downstairs and managed to sneak the phone back on its base without her noticing.

Seconds later, Dad came in and grabbed it. I followed him into the study. "What's wrong with your cell?" I asked.

"Nothing. I just thought I'd try doing without my cell for a while. To keep you company in your suffering," he said. Like it wasn't his idea! "How's it going, anyway?" he asked.

"Fine."

He looked at me sideways, as if he suspected something.

"So how's it going for you?" I asked.

He made a face. "Old habits die hard and all that. I keep thinking I've lost something. Keep patting my pocket." He did it now.

I knew the feeling. "Cleo and I are doing our socials project on addiction to technology," I told him. "Can I interview you about your withdrawal symptoms?"

"Me?" He held out a shaking hand. He made his head twitch, his tongue loll out of his mouth. "What withdrawal symptoms?" he asked.

"What is wrong with you?" asked Mom when I followed him into the kitchen.

"We're comparing withdrawal symptoms." Dad took the potato peeler from Mom. "I feel better with something in my hands. What about you, Daria?"

It was nice of Dad to let me know in his weird way that he understood what I was going through. I grabbed the placemats. "Me too. Who knows? I might even volunteer to do the dishes." Or not.

Chapter Fourteen

I spent so much time working on the project with Cleo over the next week that I barely had time to connect with Selena or Josie.

Sometimes, as Cleo and I hung out comparing notes or talking about school or movies or books, I sensed what things might have been like before TV and phones, in the dark ages before everyone was connected by technology.

That didn't mean I didn't miss technology. My hand still searched out my phone dozens of times a day.

One afternoon, Josie called our landline. Mom listened for a moment, frowning. Then she handed me the phone. "I think you'd better talk to her," she said. "But make it short."

"I tried calling you," Josie sobbed. "I've left loads of texts."

"I don't have my phone, remember? Are you okay?"

"No. Yes. No. I don't know." She took a long, shaky breath. "It's Luca. I like him. I mean, I really like him."

"So?"

"It's just. You know boys. He seems really hot for me too. Until he's around his skateboard buddies. Then I hardly exist."

"Did you have a fight?"

"Kind of."

"What does 'kind of' mean? Did you, or didn't you?"

"He told me he hated clingy girls. I wasn't clinging, I...hang on, there's another call."

"Josie?"

She came back on the line. "That was Luca. I'm headed over there now. I'll call you later, okay?"

I stared at the phone for a second. Then I handed the phone back to Mom without saying anything and headed upstairs.

There was no point trying to figure out what that had been about. Figuring out boys was hard enough. Figuring out Josie and a boy, forget it.

Maybe there was an upside to not being in constant contact!

I reread the Project Disconnect article I had downloaded. An entire school participated, even the teachers. Some university prof published a paper on the changes the teachers had noticed. Kids talking to each other. Spending more time in the library and at after-school clubs.

When I bring it up again to Cleo the next day, she said, "Don't mention it, okay? It would be death to our popularity ratings." Popularity ratings?

I gave her the notes I got from talking to Dad. She grabbed my hands. "Look at your nails! You've bitten them so far, they're bleeding. Better add that to your list of withdrawal symptoms."

I hadn't even noticed I was doing it.

In class, Ms. Stryker checked her notes when I reported on our project. "I thought you and Cleo said you were doing homelessness."

"We changed our minds." Cleo said *we* as if it hadn't all been her idea.

"That's a pity," said Stryker. "It's an important subject."

There goes our A, I thought.

"We're doing that topic," said Sara from across the room.

"We want permission to bring in a guest speaker," added her partner Shauna.

Stryker frowned at her notes. "I have here that your project was to be about getting a first job."

"A guy called Dennis lives in the bushes behind my dad's business," Sara explained. "My dad gives him stuff sometimes. Food. Blankets, when it got cold. Dennis agreed to come in and talk to the class."

"All right, all right." Stryker held up a hand to hush the chatter. "Sara and Shauna, that's something you'll have to clear with the vice-principal. Now, can we finish with the updates and get on to other work?"

"That's what we need," said Cleo on our way out of school. "A guest speaker. Maybe we can invite your dad."

"We don't need to invite him," I told her. Like I was going to let my own father stand up in front of my classmates! I was almost as surprised as Cleo when the words came out of my mouth. "I can be the guest speaker."

"What do you mean?"

"We'll present our report, like we planned. And then I'll tell everyone what gave us the idea for the project."

"That's already part of the introduction."

"Not just about having my phone confiscated. But why."

She took a step back and stared at me. "Like, about Caden? I thought you didn't want to go into specifics."

"We were going to use case studies anyway. The one about the guy who stepped into traffic because he was so busy on his phone. And the girl who didn't hear the truck backing up when she was plugged into her iPod."

"That's different. No one knows those people," said Cleo. "But they know you."

"If we put a face to the risks, it will have more impact, won't it? Like having a real live homeless person is sure to get everyone's attention."

"I guess that's one way to make friends and influence people!" Cleo looked doubtful. "I can't figure out if you are brave, stupid or suicidal."

Chapter Fifteen

The class yawned through much of Sara and Shauna's PowerPoint statistics on homelessness. But they sat up and took notice when Dennis shuffled into the room.

It was probably the first time most of us had seen a homeless person up close. His coat was worn, his jeans were rolled up a couple of times and one of his runners had holes in it. I could smell him from where I sat. He told us about the accountant's job he lost after he got sick, about the family he lost when he turned to drink and drugs. Even though his eyes were bloodshot, his face sallow and his hair greasy, he spoke like a professor or a doctor. He sounded educated and had a big vocabulary.

"That's a hard act to follow," said Cleo as Sara and Shauna showed him out. She pushed the thumb drive with our presentation into the laptop.

"All set?" asked Stryker. "We still have three more presentations to get through today."

"We're good." Cleo hit a key. The screen went blank. "Hang on," she said. "This should work." She hit another key.

Nothing.

"I'll get it." I leaned across to help.

She elbowed me aside. "No. Hang on. It can't be that hard." She slapped random keys, twiddled with the focus on the projector. "It worked a minute ago. Shauna must have done something to mess things up." Cleo bit her lip so hard, I expected the ring to pop out. She yanked her hat on tighter and rubbed her bright red face with her hand. "How hard can it be?"

"It's fine," I told her. "Let me get it going."

"Go ahead, then. You're the technology whiz." She stomped back to her seat.

But by now, the laptop had frozen and the projection screen was blank.

"Can I help?" Ms. Stryker fiddled with all the knobs. But she could not bring the setup back to life.

"You could try rebooting the laptop," said Drew.

"I'll reboot you," Cleo muttered, loud enough for everyone to hear.

Stryker checked her watch. "Time's a-wasting here," she said. "Perhaps you would prefer to present with tomorrow's group."

"It's fine. I have copies of the slides here," I told the class. "We can work from these."

"Cleo, are you going to come up and present with Daria?" asked Ms. Stryker.

"I'm fine," she muttered. "Daria's fine. Go ahead, why don't you?"

I got through our presentation without too much stumbling. Most people listened. Some threw out a remark or two.

"Cleo, how about you join Daria for a quick Q and A?" Ms. Stryker said as I slid the prompt sheets into their folder when I was done. "I can give you two minutes."

"As long as I don't have to touch that projector thingy again," said Cleo as she sidled up to stand next to me.

A few friendly laughs went around the room.

"There's a bit more background I need to share," I said. Having Cleo standing there encouraged me to go on. "We've given you the facts." It had been *me*, not *we* actually. But I wasn't about to quibble. "About some of the effects of dependence on technology. But I want to tell you why my phone was confiscated for a whole month. Why I am disconnected for another two and a half weeks. Eighteen days to be exact, but who's counting?" I cleared my throat and glanced at Cleo.

She smiled and nodded.

"I had a babysitting job. So I could earn the fare to visit my old friends in Calgary. One day, when I was on the phone—" My voice trembled. I took a deep breath. "The little boy I was babysitting, Caden, he fell off the bed and bashed his head. He knocked himself out. There was blood everywhere." My voice sounded very loud. "He could have died," I said. "Because I was not paying attention. My parents confiscated my phone, and I got fired. A little boy nearly died. Because of me."

As I was wondering how I could get out of there, Harrison asked from the back row, "So what happened to the kid?"

Everyone turned to look at him, then back at me.

"He'll be all right." I touched the back of my hair. "But he had to have twenty-one stitches in his head."

Some students gasped. Others muttered.

"But he's fine now," Cleo added quickly.

Harrison clapped. Other students joined in.

I dropped the handouts on the desk. "Our presentation is about the effects of dependence on technology," I said. "But you probably know all about it already. In fact, I bet right now most of you can't wait for class to be over so you can check your messages. That's how dependent you all are."

There was lots of shuffling and nervous laughter.

"Some schools in the States did something called Project Disconnect," I went on quickly. "The school banned all devices. For a whole month. Not even teachers could use them on school time. Can you imagine! We don't have to go that far, maybe. But perhaps my story—and our project—is enough to make everyone think about their preoccupation with technology."

"That's it, folks," said Cleo. "Send your questions by carrier pigeon, if you have any!"

"Thank you, girls." Ms. Stryker tapped my arm as I went back to my desk. "I'd be interested in knowing more about Project Disconnect."

A couple of students groaned as I handed her the printout.

"I wonder if this might be worth considering as a class project," said Ms. Stryker. "What do you all think?"

The room erupted in jeers and cross talk.

"I'm in." Cleo's voice cut through the noise. "Who's with me?"

There was laughter. Some from the back called out, "You're kidding, right?"

"You don't even have a phone," Drew said.

"You can't even make a PowerPoint work!" jeered someone else.

"Maybe I can't," said Cleo. "Maybe I don't," she told Drew. "But what about you, Mr. Chess Champion? Are you up for it?"

"I've got a chess app on my phone," he said. "There's an important tournament coming up."

"Fine. What about you, Harrison?" Cleo asked.

Now, *he* had a nice face, I noticed.

"Okay, okay," Drew interrupted. "But just for one week. One week and no more."

"I'm in too." Harrison pulled his phone from his pocket. He made a big deal of turning it off and dropping it into his bag.

Ms. Stryker watched without speaking as one student after another signed on.

Some of them volunteered on their own, others were bullied into it. Peer pressure at work, I thought as Cleo picked out the kids trying to pretend they were not in the room.

I confronted a girl who was texting under her desk. "You in, Madison?" I asked. "Or are you going to be one of the holdouts?"

When Madison saw everyone staring at her, she slammed down her phone. "Okay. Okay. Now get out of my face."

"That was interesting. And enlightening," said Ms. Stryker. "I'll spend a bit of time with this, do some of my own research. I'll figure out how this might work. But for now, we have a few more projects to get through."

Cleo turned toward me and raised her hand.

We high-fived.

"That has to get us an A," she said.

Chapter Sixteen

Cleo was wrong.

"An impressive piece of work." Dad read Stryker's comment below the A-minus on the report.

"We deserved an A," Cleo said for the hundredth time.

"And we might have got one if we hadn't screwed up on the PowerPoint presentation," I said, being careful not to look at her.

"That's right. Blame it on me." When she shook her head, the strings on her hat flailed around her head.

"Didn't your teacher tell you that you lost points because you depended on technology for a project on technology dependence? Not because you couldn't make it work?" asked Mom.

"Isn't that the same thing?" I asked.

"No. It's not," said Cleo. "Besides, we would have aced the project with a better speaker. I'm not saying you didn't do a great job," she said when she saw the look on my face. "But Dennis DeVos stood out. You, you're just one of the crowd."

I was, I realized. It had taken a few weeks—and hanging out with Cleo—to feel like I actually belonged here.

"A-minus is a good grade," said Dad. "Technology aside, it sounds like you both did a great job."

"To recognize your hard work on this, perhaps we could help with the fare to Calgary for spring break," said Mom.

Dad nodded.

"Dee and I have plans," said Cleo. "With a couple of other kids from school."

Who knew that hanging out with Drew Galling could be a blast? Especially with Harrison making up the fourth. It turned out he was more than just a nice face.

"Dee?" asked Dad. "Daria is Dee now?"

"Cleo thinks it suits me."

"I guess I'll get used to it." He left the room muttering, "Whatever is next? Piercings?"

He came back right away with my phone. "I think you've earned this back. I'm sure you've learned from all your

recent research. Don't you think?"
he asked Mom.

I reached for the phone. Four weeks
had sounded like such a long time.

Cleo grabbed it first. "It's nicer than
mine."

"You don't have a phone!" I said.

"Do too! I finally convinced Mom
and Dad that they can't live in the
dark ages forever." She passed me my
phone and rooted in her bag. "See?"
The phone she held out was an old one,
as big as a brick. It probably dated back
to pioneer times. "Recycled," she said.
"As you might expect." She grinned
at me. "Now we can connect anytime,
unless Stryker has her way."

Dad smiled slyly at me. "Oh. I'm
sure clever girls like you can work
something out."

Did he know I had cheated? If so,
there was no sign from Mom that he had
told her.

While Cleo pressed buttons on her phone, I picked up mine from the table. It fitted my hand, as if it belonged there. I couldn't help it. I turned it on.

Nineteen calls. Texts galore. My fingers itched to scroll through them.

Then I looked at Mom and Dad. They were frowning as they watched Cleo punch the keys of her phone, shake it, hold it up to her ear, glare at it.

I put my phone on the counter.

First call I would make would be to Cynthia. Maybe she would let me speak to Caden and Emerson to see if Caden's hair was growing back and find out how Emmy did with her science project.

I could connect with Josie and Selena later.

I headed to the fridge for the tiramisu Cleo and I had made earlier. While we had mixed and poured, I had told her about the Cool Code of Conduct. She'd asked, "And how has that worked out for you lately?" All I could do was laugh.

She was still fiddling with her phone as I put dessert on the table and passed out forks. "Put that down," I told Cleo. "I'll help you figure it out later. But first, let's eat."

Lois Peterson wrote short stories and articles for adults for twenty years before turning to writing for kids. She was born in England and has lived in Iraq, France and the United States. She works at a plublic library and lives in Surrey, British Columbia, where she writes, reads and teaches creative writing to adults, teens and children. Lois is the author of several books for children and youth, including *Beyond Repair* in the Orca Currents series.

Titles in the Series

orca currents